SIX EXCITING ADVENTURES

Thomas the Tank Engine

Story Treasury

DEAN

First published in Great Britain in 2021 by Dean, part of Farshore
An imprint of HarperCollins*Publishers*
1 London Bridge Street, London SE1 9GF
www.farshore.co.uk

HarperCollins*Publishers*
1st Floor, Watermarque Building, Ringsend Road
Dublin 4, Ireland

The Story of Thomas the Tank Engine first published in 2015, written by Ronne Randall,
based on *Thomas the Tank Engine* first published in Great Britain in 1946
A Visit to London for Thomas the Tank Engine first published in 2016, written by Ronne Randall
Three Cheers for Thomas the Tank Engine first published in 2015, written by Joseph Marriott and Jane Riordan
Thomas and the Spring Surprise first published in 2019, written by Emily Stead and Helen Archer
Thomas and the Dinosaurs first published in 2019, written by Jane Riordan
Thomas goes on Safari first published in 2020, written by Katrina Pallant

Designed by Martin Aggett
Stories illustrated by Robin Davies
Map illustration by Dan Crisp

CREATED BY BRITT ALLCROFT

Based on the Railway Series by the Reverend W Awdry. © 2021 Gullane (Thomas) Limited.
Thomas the Tank Engine & Friends™ and Thomas & Friends™ are trademarks of Gullane (Thomas) Limited.
© 2021 HIT Entertainment Limited. HIT and the HIT logo are trademarks of HIT Entertainment Limited.

ISBN 978 0 0085 0927 9
Printed in China
001

A CIP catalogue record for this title is available from the British Library.

Stay safe online. Farshore is not responsible for content hosted by third parties.

Farshore takes its responsibility to the planet and its inhabitants very seriously.
We aim to use papers from well-managed forests run by responsible suppliers.

Thomas the Tank Engine

Story Treasury

THE STORY OF
Thomas the Tank Engine

This is a story about Thomas the Tank Engine, who worked with his engine friends on The Fat Controller's Railway on the Island of Sodor.

Thomas the Tank Engine was a cheeky little engine who helped the big engines by pulling their coaches to and from the **BIG** Station.

But what Thomas really wanted was his very own Branch Line. That way he would be a **Really Useful Engine.**

9

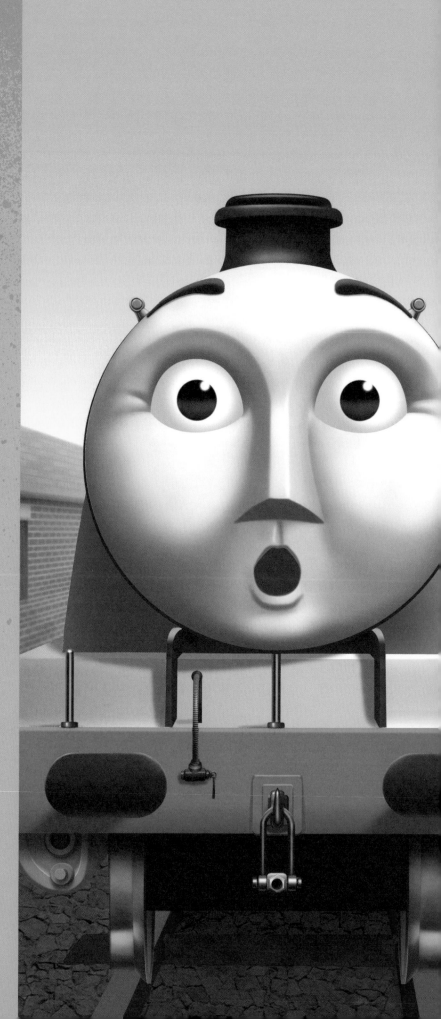

Sometimes Thomas liked to play tricks on the other engines.

One day, when Gordon, the **BIG STRONG** engine, was very tired from pulling the heavy Express train, Thomas came up beside him and whistled loudly.

"PEEP! PEEP!

WAKE UP, LAZYBONES!"

That gave Gordon a fright! He decided to teach cheeky Thomas a lesson.

The next morning, Thomas would not wake up. It was nearly time for Gordon's Express to leave, and Thomas hadn't got his coaches ready.

"Yaa-aaw-n," said Thomas, getting started at last.

"Hurry up, Thomas!" said Gordon crossly.

Thomas' job was to push Gordon's train to help him start.

As he moved out of the station, he started to go *faster* and *faster*.

Faster and *faster* and *faster* and *faster* went Gordon.

It was much too *fast* for Thomas!

That morning was Gordon's chance to teach Thomas a lesson.

"Hurry, hurry, hurry, hurry!" laughed Gordon.

Poor Thomas was going **faster** than he had ever gone before.

"My wheels will wear out!" he thought.

"Peep!
Peep!
Stop! Stop!"

whistled Thomas.

At last they stopped at a station.

"Well, Thomas," chuckled Gordon. "Now you know how it feels to be tricked!"

"Puff! Puff!" panted poor Thomas.

He was too out of breath to say anything.
His cheekiness had got him into trouble.
Perhaps he would never get his
own Branch Line now.

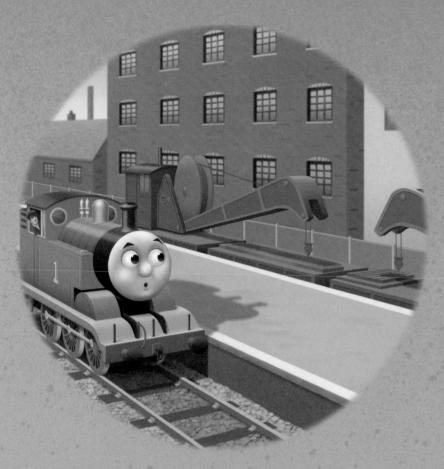

The next day, Thomas saw some strange-looking trucks in the Yard.

"That's the breakdown train," said his Driver. "It helps out when there's an accident."

Just then, James, the Splendid Red Engine, came through the Yard crying.

His trucks were pushing him too *fast*, and his brake blocks were on fire!

"HELP!

HELP!"

Soon after James disappeared, a man came running.

"James is off the line! We need the breakdown train – quickly!" he shouted.

Thomas was coupled on to the breakdown train, and off he went as **fast** as he could.

Whirrrrr went his wheels along the track.

"I must help James," he said.

They found James in a field, with the trucks piled in a heap behind him. His Driver and Fireman were checking that he was all right.

"It wasn't your fault, James," his Driver said.
"It was those Troublesome Trucks!"

James needed help. Thomas pushed the breakdown train alongside James.

Then he pulled some trucks out of the way.

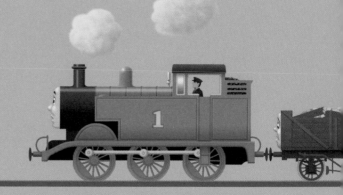

He was soon back to pick up the rest.

"Oh... dear! Oh... dear!"

they groaned.

"Serves you right. Serves you right," puffed Thomas crossly. He worked hard all afternoon.

Thomas pulled James back to the Shed, where The Fat Controller was waiting.

"Well, Thomas," he said, "you have shown that you're a **Really Useful Engine**. I'm so pleased with you that I'm going to give you your own Branch Line."

"Oh, thank you, Sir!"
said Thomas happily.

Now Thomas is happy as can be, and he **chuffs** and **puffs** proudly along his own Branch Line from morning till night.

Gordon is always in a hurry, but whenever he sees Thomas he remembers to say, **"Hurry! Hurry!"** And cheeky little Thomas always whistles,

"PEEP! PEEP!

Lazybones!"

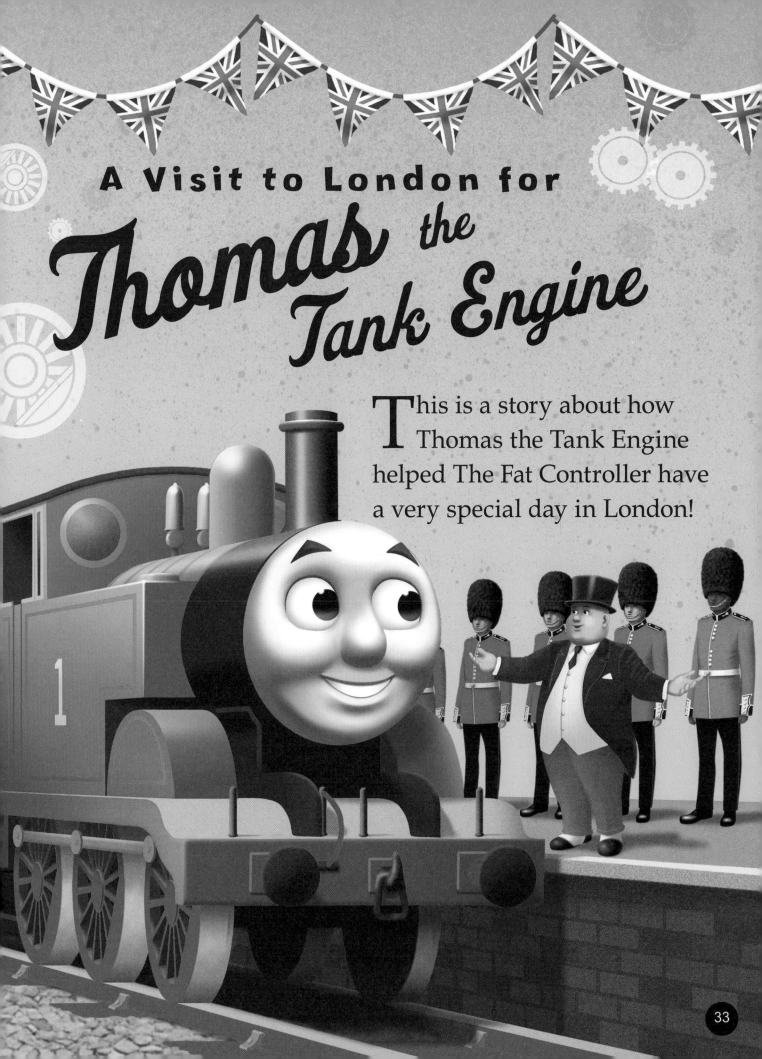

A Visit to London for Thomas the Tank Engine

This is a story about how Thomas the Tank Engine helped The Fat Controller have a very special day in London!

Thomas the Tank Engine and Henry, Gordon and Edward were all shiny and polished. Their Drivers wanted them to look their best.

The Fat Controller was going to choose one of them to do a very special job!

The Fat Controller
inspected each engine.

Finally he announced, "Thomas, I choose you to take me and Lady Hatt to London to meet the **Queen!** We must get to Big Ben at four o'clock for the start of her birthday celebrations."

None of the engines were sure who Big Ben was but Thomas shivered with excitement. He would be meeting the Queen and going to London, the biggest city in the land!

The next morning, Thomas was coupled up to Annie, who carried The Fat Controller and Lady Hatt.

They chugged off to Brendam Docks, where Cranky was waiting to put them on the ferry to the Mainland.

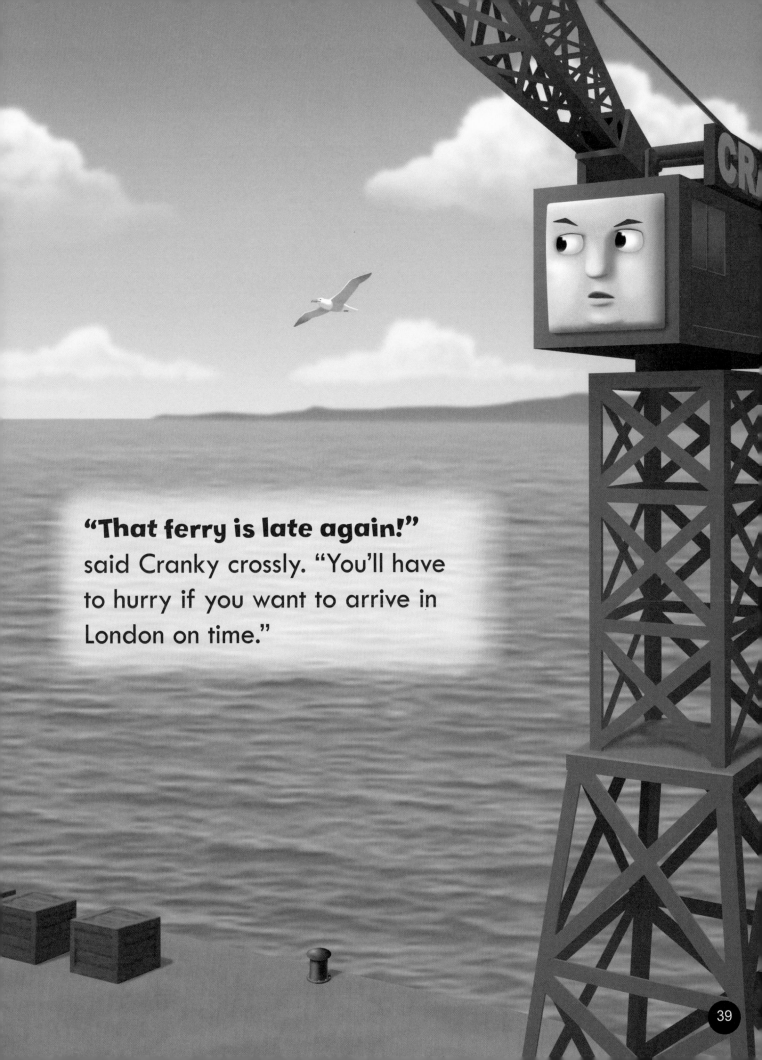

"That ferry is late again!" said Cranky crossly. "You'll have to hurry if you want to arrive in London on time."

On the Mainland, Thomas
puffed through the countryside...

...and past a big train going the other way.
"Peep! Peep!" called Thomas.
"Wheeeeeeeee!" the train whistled back.

"Mustn't be late! Mustn't be late!"
Thomas puffed. "It's already two o'clock."

"Hurry! Hurry! Hurry!" he panted as, at last, roofs and chimneys came into sight.

"Good work, Thomas!" said his Driver.
"We've arrived in Greenwich. That building is
the Royal Observatory. They have a telescope
there that can see all the way to the stars!"

"Can it see as far as Sodor?"
Thomas asked.

"Much further!" laughed his Driver.

At the River Thames, Thomas was told that they would be finishing the journey by boat.

Thomas saw a big sailing ship. "Is that the boat?" he wondered.

"No," said his Driver, smiling. "That is a very old ship called the *Cutty Sark*. It used to bring tea all the way from China."

Thomas had never heard about so many faraway places in just one day!

All at once there was a merry **TOOT! TOOT!**

"I'm Dilly," said a friendly barge. "I'll take you into London and show you some sights along the way!"

"It's three o'clock," Thomas said nervously. "We mustn't be late for the Queen and Big Ben!"

"I'll have you there quicker than you can say 'Piccadilly Circus!'" Dilly promised.

With Thomas and Annie safely aboard, Dilly set off. A big bridge loomed up in front of them. To Thomas' amazement, it opened up to let them through!

"This is Tower Bridge," Dilly told him. "And there is the Tower of London. It's almost a thousand years old!"

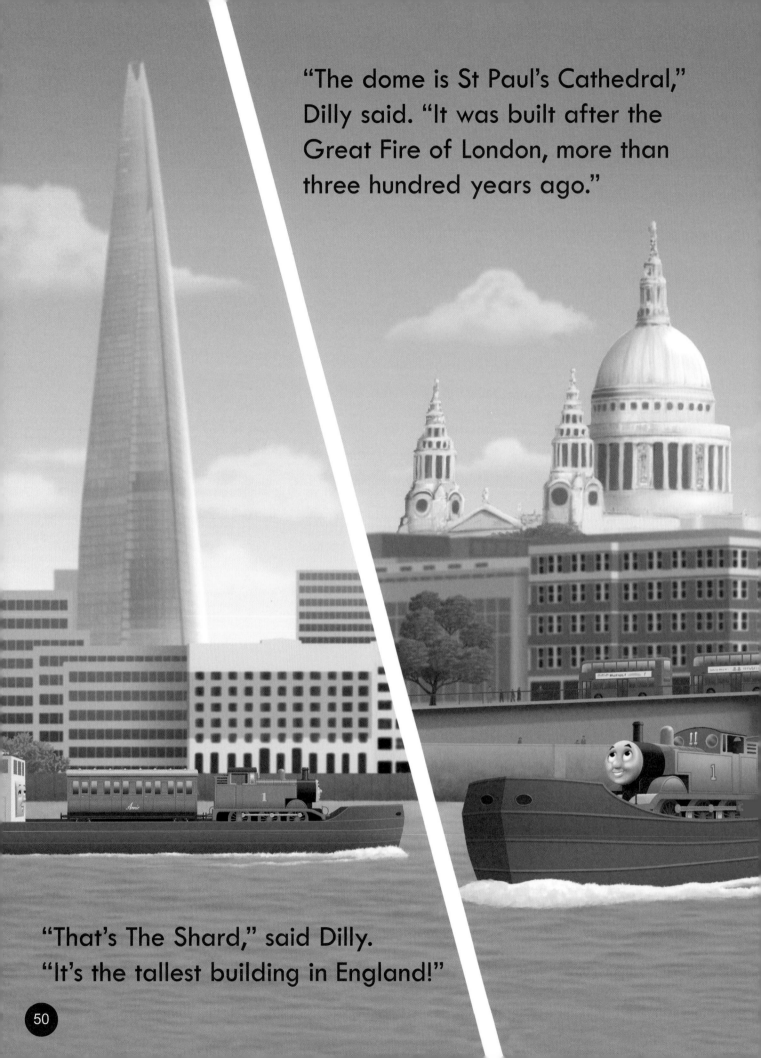

"The dome is St Paul's Cathedral," Dilly said. "It was built after the Great Fire of London, more than three hundred years ago."

"That's The Shard," said Dilly.
"It's the tallest building in England!"

"That big wheel is the London Eye," Dilly went on. "From the top you can see all over London!"

51

"These are the Houses of Parliament," Dilly explained. "This is where laws are made. And there is the Elizabeth Tower, with its huge bell, Big Ben."

Suddenly there was a loud
BONG! BONG! BONG! BONG!

"Four o'clock!" said Dilly. "We're right on time!"

"So that's Big Ben," laughed Thomas looking up at the big clock.

As Dilly pulled up at Westminster, the Royal party came out onto the terrace.

The Queen thanked The Fat Controller for running such a fine Railway.

"I couldn't do it without Thomas and my other Really Useful Engines," replied The Fat Controller.

Thomas beamed from buffer to buffer.

That evening, as Thomas, Annie and Dilly rested on the Thames, brilliant fireworks lit up the sky.

CRACKLE! WHOOOOSHH! BOOM!

Thomas couldn't wait to tell his friends on Sodor about Big Ben, meeting the Queen and everything he'd seen in the biggest city in the land.

THREE CHEERS FOR
Thomas
the Tank Engine

One sunny day on the Island of Sodor, Thomas was running late.

"Go faster, go faster!" grumbled his coaches, Annie and Clarabel.

"I'm trying, I'm trying," puffed Thomas, but his wheels felt all wrong — they were stiff and sore.

The next day was no better.
Thomas was late to be coupled up to Annie and Clarabel...

late delivering
goods trucks...

late shunting trucks...

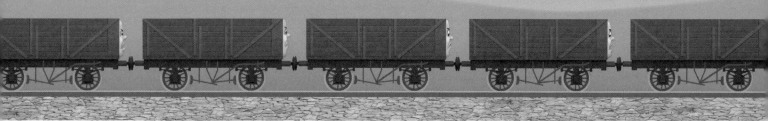

...and late to the Washdown at the end of the day.

It was the same story all week.

Normally Thomas loved to race with his friend Bertie the Bus but on this day Thomas was too tired and his wheels were too sore to rush about.

"Not today, Bertie,"

said Thomas.

That night, Thomas puffed back to the Sheds, very slowly and very sadly.

Everyone was worried about Thomas. He was normally such a **cheerful little engine.** Nobody liked seeing him so sad.

"I remember when I had my **old, rusty pipes,**" said James. "I felt so slow and tired. I used to get out of breath, even on the shortest journey."

67

So the Engines decided to talk to The Fat Controller to see what could be done.

"Thomas' wheels are **rusty and worn**,"
The Fat Controller said. "We'll give him a
special day with new paint, new wheels
and a **surprise party** to celebrate!"

"With new wheels, Thomas
might be *faster* than you,
Bertie," teased Emily.

"Never!"
tooted Bertie.

The next day The Fat Controller went to see Thomas.

"Today," he said, "you won't be pulling Annie and Clarabel. I'm sending you to the **Sodor Steamworks**."

"I understand," thought Thomas, sadly. "I'm not good enough to pull coaches. I'm not a Really Useful Engine."

And he **puffed** off to the Steamworks feeling very sorry for himself.

But at the Steamworks Thomas was given a smart **new coat of paint**...

...his dome was **polished**...

...his buffers were **buffed**...

...and he was given **brand new, shiny wheels!**

Thomas was about to puff off to his party at Knapford Station when Bertie pulled up next to him.

"Let's race to the party!"

Bertie said. "It's time to test out those special new wheels."

Bertie pulled away **more quickly** than Thomas and took the lead.

But Thomas' new wheels were turning *faster* and *faster* and *faster*.

He was catching up.

And when Bertie stopped to let some ducks cross the road, *Thomas overtook him!*

"Three cheers for Thomas!" said The Fat Controller, as they arrived first at the party.

"Hip hip hooray! Hip hip hooray! Hip hip hooray!"

"I just couldn't keep up with those new wheels," Bertie said as he pulled up.

79

It was a **wonderful party**! All Thomas' friends congratulated him on winning the race. Then they admired his new coat of paint and his shiny new wheels.

"Peep! Peep!"
Thomas tooted happily.

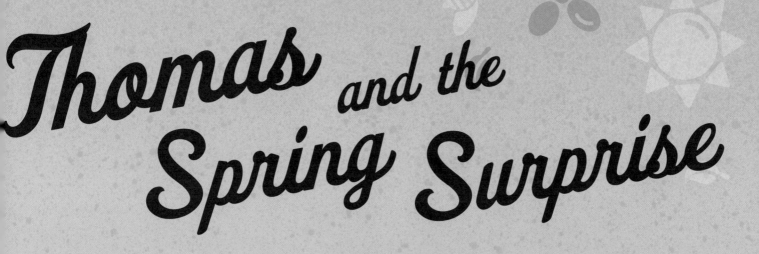

Thomas and the Spring Surprise

This is a story about a spring day when lambs were born on the farm and Thomas was given the chance to show what a Really Useful Engine he was …

One of Thomas' favourite things to do is to visit the farm. He loves to see Farmer McColl's sheep grazing in their field.

"Baa! Baa!"
the sheep would call.

"Peep! Peep!"
Thomas would whistle back.

One day, when Thomas was passing the field, Farmer McColl waved him over.

"Hello, Thomas!" said Farmer McColl. "I'm glad you're here. I have very special news. Some lambs are going to be born today."

Thomas was very excited.

"I can't wait to meet them!" he peeped.

"Newborn lambs need to have fresh straw," Farmer McColl explained. "Can you go to the old barn at Maron to collect some?"

"Right away!"

Thomas puffed, and off he went to the old barn.

Thomas wondered if there was anything else the lambs would like.

On his way, Thomas passed the bakery. He saw Percy loading his truck with freshly-baked bread.

"Maybe the lambs would like some bread," he puffed. "Percy, may I have some?"

"Of course!" said Percy and his crew loaded trays of bread into Thomas' truck.

Thomas steamed on cheerily, until he came to the garden centre where he saw James picking up colourful spring flowers.

Thomas was sure the lambs would like the flowers.

"May I have some for the lambs?"
Thomas asked, and James agreed.

Thomas was nearly at the old barn when he saw Charlie waiting at a signal.

"Hello, Charlie!" puffed Thomas. "I'm going to meet some newborn lambs today!"

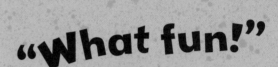

"What fun!" chuffed Charlie. "I'm going to the dairy to collect cheese."

Thomas thought that the lambs might like cheese too, so he went with Charlie to have some cheese loaded into his truck.

After the dairy, Thomas hurried on to the old barn to collect the straw.

"Your truck is full," the farm worker said. **"There's no room for the straw."**

"Fizzling fireboxes!" Thomas exclaimed. "I'll just have to take the lambs the bread, cheese and flowers instead."

When Thomas returned to the farm, Farmer McColl was not happy to see there was no straw in the truck. "The lambs must have straw to keep them warm," he said. **"And they'll be born before the sun goes down!"**

Thomas felt very silly. "I'm sorry. I will go and collect the straw straight away!" he peeped.

Thomas raced back to the old barn, saying over and over to himself, "I must get the straw, there can be no delay. The lambs will be born by the end of the day!"

He **steamed** past Percy, refilling at the water tower, **whizzed** past James at a junction and Charlie at the station. There was no time to stop!

The sun was setting when Thomas arrived at the old barn.

"Hello again!" Thomas puffed to the Farm Worker. "Please can you load the straw into my truck? I must get it to the lambs before they get cold!"

The farm worker quickly loaded the straw bales and soon Thomas was on his way back to the farm.

Thomas steamed so quickly, his axles ached. "I must go fast, I mustn't delay. The lambs must have straw by the end of the day!" he sang.

When he reached the farm, he was so worried he would be too late.

"You're just in time," Farmer McColl smiled. **"The lambs have just been born!"**

Thomas was delighted he had arrived in time to meet the lambs.

The next day, Thomas took some school children to visit the new little lambs.

Farmer McColl laid out the bread, cheese and flowers and the children had a splendid spring picnic.

"I have a **surprise** for you, Thomas," smiled Farmer McColl. "I named this lamb **'Thomas'** ... after you!"

"Peep! Peep!"

Thomas whistled, happily.

"Baa! Baa!"

the lambs answered.

Thomas and the Dinosaurs

This is the story about Thomas the Tank Engine and the time he came face to face with a dinosaur …

Thomas the Tank Engine liked to boast that he wasn't scared of anything.

"Nothing scares me," he peeped to his coaches Annie and Clarabel. They just smiled. They were used to Thomas showing off!

James was taking some passengers to the Docks.

"Peep! Peep!" tooted Thomas, as he sped past.

"Made you jump!" laughed Thomas as he disappeared into the distance.

James was **not** pleased.

But Thomas was having
too much fun.

"I'm going to give Percy
a scare," he laughed to
himself, when he saw Percy
resting in the Sheds.

"Peep! Peep!"
Percy was jolted wide awake.
He was **not** pleased.

That evening, The Fat Controller had an important job for Thomas.

He needed him to work through the night, delivering supplies to the Workmen.

The sun had set and ...

as the stars came out, the shadows darkened ...

Thomas had never been out so late before and he'd never seen Sodor looking so dark before. As he arrived at the Docks, he saw the **huge** shadow of Cranky the Crane looming over him. It gave him quite a fright but then he saw something even more terrifying …

Out at sea, a horned creature seemed to be attacking a ship!

Thomas didn't wait to see what happened next.

"Help! Help!" he puffed, as he steamed

back to the Engine Sheds.

But James and Percy wouldn't listen to Thomas.

"You're just trying to scare us again," they cried.

Thomas didn't sleep at all well that night.

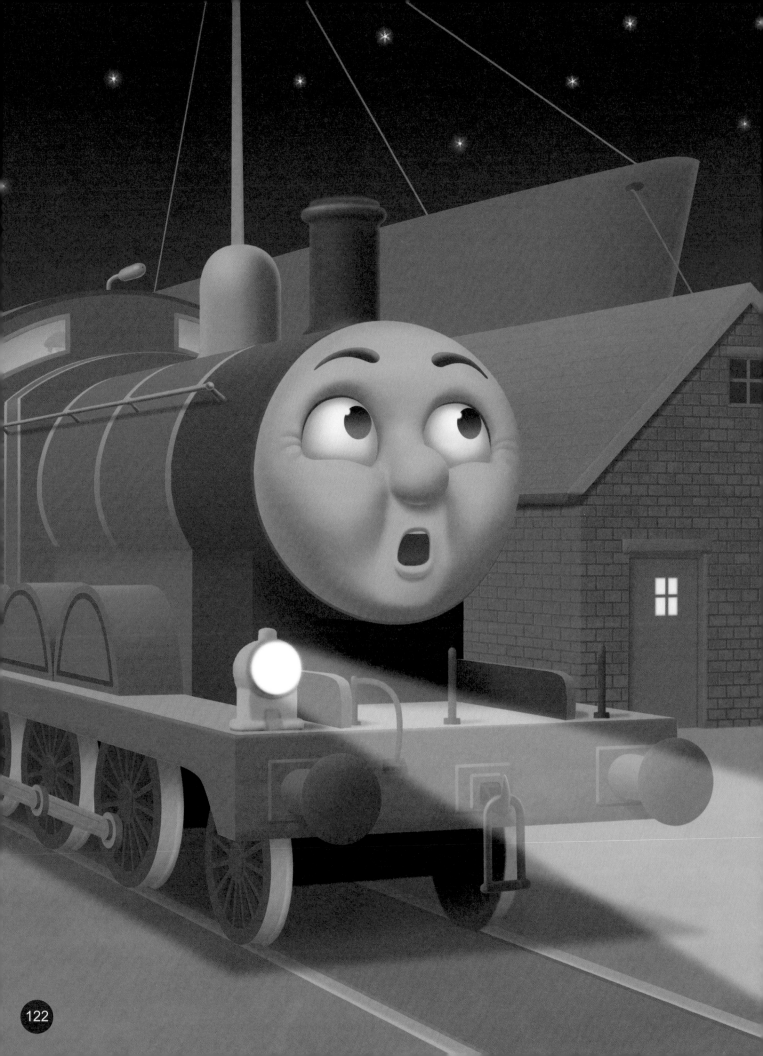

The next night it was James who was sent out to make deliveries.

As he went past the Docks, he caught sight of a **gigantic** mouth, full of sharp teeth.

"Help! Help!"

he puffed, as he *wheeshed* away from the monster, as fast as he could.

Percy had heard Thomas and James's tales of **monsters**, but he didn't believe them.

"They're just trying to scare me," he said to himself, **bravely,** as he set out the next evening to deliver the night mail.

But as he got close to the Docks, a **huge** shadow fell across the tracks ...

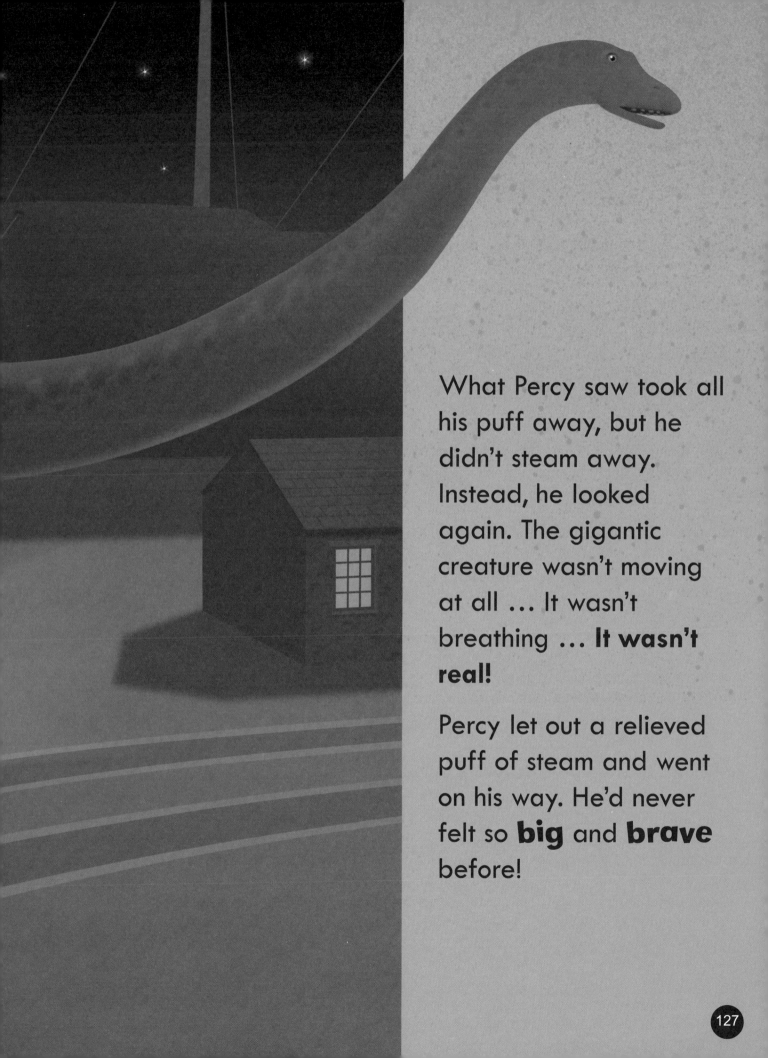

What Percy saw took all his puff away, but he didn't steam away. Instead, he looked again. The gigantic creature wasn't moving at all … It wasn't breathing … **It wasn't real!**

Percy let out a relieved puff of steam and went on his way. He'd never felt so **big** and **brave** before!

The next morning, The Fat Controller went to speak to the engines.

"I've heard that some of you have had a scare," he smiled.

Thomas and James blushed from buffer to buffer.

"The creatures you've seen in the night aren't anything to be scared of," he explained. "They're models for the new Dinosaur Park."

The engines were excited to hear about the park.

"Thomas, Percy and James, I'd like you to deliver the dinosaurs," announced The Fat Controller. **"If you're not too scared, that is!"**

The engines worked hard all day.

... then the fierce **Tyrannosaurus** ...

... and finally, the long-tailed **Diplodocus** were delivered to

First the horned **Triceratops** ...

their new home in the Dinosaur Park.

DINOSAUR

6

The next day, the Dinosaur Park was open to the public. Thomas was put in charge of taking the very first visitors to see the dinosaurs.

The children **squealed** and **shouted** with terrified delight.

DINOSAUR PARK

"There's nothing to be scared of,"
Thomas reassured them.

Percy overheard Thomas and chuckled to himself!

Thomas goes on Safari

This is a story about Thomas, the brave blue engine, and the day he went on an adventure very far from home …

Thomas was getting ready for a busy day on Sodor when the Fat Controller arrived with some news.

"Thomas, I have a very special job for you this week. You are going to travel to Africa to work with Nia on the Kenyan railway. She has gone on ahead so you will meet her there."

"How exciting!" Thomas thought.

Thomas **puffed** through Sodor on his way to the Docks ...

... where Dilly the Barge was waiting
to transport him across the ocean.

After a long journey, Thomas arrived on the
continent of Africa and headed to Kenya.

Thomas was happy to have arrived at last.

"Hello Thomas!" Nia shouted, as Thomas pulled up. "We are going on a practice run before taking passengers on safari! Hopefully we will see some lions and elephants in their natural habitat."

Thomas knew he should be excited, but he was worried. Weren't elephants **really big?** Didn't lions have **pointed, scary teeth?**

"Don't be scared, Thomas," Nia said. "We'll start with gentle giraffes."

Thomas and Nia rolled quietly along the track, through the Kenyan animal reserve, until they spotted a group of giraffes eating leaves.

Thomas stared up in wonder at the tallest creatures he'd ever seen.

"Giraffes can grow to **6 metres tall**," Nia explained. "That's taller than a double-decker bus!"

Thomas and Nia rolled on visiting the animals on the reserve

Thomas couldn't believe it when Nia told him zebras could run up to **65 kilometres** per hour. Faster than Bertie the bus!

"Did you know elephants can drink over **200 litres** of water per day?" Nia said. Almost as much as fills a swimming pool!

Nia warned Thomas that visitors should not get too close to the rhinos.

Thomas was amazed by all the different animals, but he was still worried about the **roaring** lions and **big** elephants.

Just then, a giant hippo appeared out of the river with a ...

Splash!

Thomas was scared. He imagined the hippo was coming after him. He **peeped** his whistle and sped away up the track.

Nia **chugged** after Thomas. She tried to tell him that the hippo wasn't chasing him.

But it was too late. Thomas rolled so fast up the track that he didn't see the trouble ahead.

There had been a landslide and now Thomas was **stuck in the mud!**

"Why did you go so fast, Thomas?" Nia asked when she arrived. "Not to worry, I'll go and get the towrope to pull you out."

"Sorry, Nia. I was scared and went too fast."
Thomas was embarrassed.

But instead of digging Thomas out, Nia's crew started putting more mud on him. "On hot days, hippos coat themselves in mud," Nia explained. "This will keep you cool while I fetch help."

When Nia returned to tow Thomas out of the mud, he was **dirtier than he had ever been!**

"I stayed nice and cool thanks to your idea with the mud," Thomas said. "Those hippos are clever."

Nia pulled him free and took him to be
washed down by a friendly elephant.
Thomas was no longer scared of this
giant but gentle creature.

Nia took Thomas back to the river to show him a family of hippos. He realised they weren't scary either, as long as you didn't get too close!

"There is a lot **we can learn** from the animals if we pay attention," replied Nia.

After their practice run, Nia and Thomas took lots of passengers on safari. Everyone had a great time and Thomas even conquered his fear of lions!

The engines were ready to head home. "I've learned more about the animals and I hope to come again soon," Thomas said. He peeped goodbye to Kenya.

157